Jack's Plan

Margaret Clyne

Illustrated by Trish Hill

CELEBRATION PRESS

Pearson Learning Group

Jack went to stay with
his Grandma.

His Grandma ran
an inn.

That afternoon Jack
helped Grandma set up
for breakfast the next day.

"After breakfast
tomorrow, we'll take
Daisy and go to the
park," said Grandma.

The next morning Jack
got up at half past seven.
"Has everyone had
breakfast yet?"
asked Jack.

"No," said Grandma.
So Jack had some cereal.

Jack looked at the clock.
It was eight o'clock.
"Haven't they all had
breakfast yet?" asked Jack.

"No," said Grandma.
So Jack had some milk.

Jack looked at the clock.
It was half past eight.
"Haven't they all had
breakfast yet?" asked Jack.

"No," said Grandma.
So Jack had some toast.

At nine o'clock it began
to rain.

"We'll have to go
to the park tomorrow,"
said Grandma.
So Jack made a plan.

The next morning Jack
got up at half past seven.

He ran to all the rooms
and banged and banged
on all the doors.
"Breakfast time," he yelled,
"breakfast time!"

Everyone came down
for breakfast at
eight o'clock.
"Now we can go to the
park before it rains,"
said Jack.